Alan
and his
Perfectly
Pointy
Impossibly
Perpendicular
Pinky

by Alan Page and Kamie Page
artwork by David Geister

Alan
and his
Perfectly
Pointy
Impossibly
Perpendicular
Pinky

PAGE EDUCATION
FOUNDATION
MINNEAPOLIS, MINNESOTA

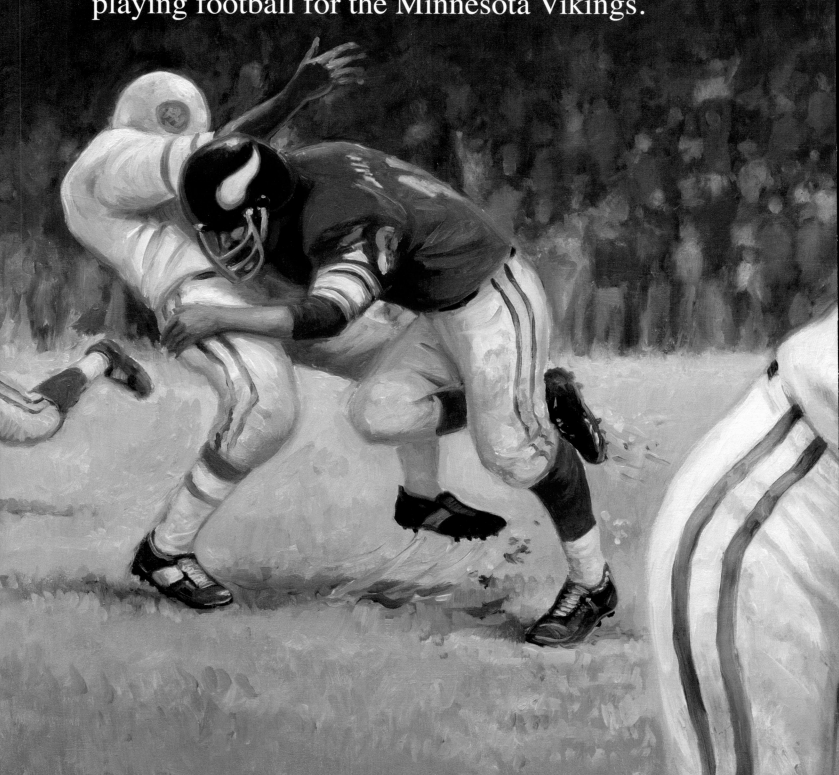

Alan Page has big hands. His scarred fingers twist and turn from tackles made and touchdowns prevented when playing football for the Minnesota Vikings.

His palms are calloused from the years of gripping his gavel on the bench as a State Supreme Court Justice.

Though his hands may not look soft, Alan's grandchildren don't seem to mind when he snuggles up with them to read a story, or gently wipe away a tear.

But the most curious thing about Alan's hands is his **perfectly pointy impossibly perpendicular pinky**.

Today as Alan looked at his hands while tying his favorite bowtie, he thought about his plans for the morning.

You see, Alan loves to spend time talking with and reading to young children, and today was a special day. He was heading back to Market Elementary School, where he first learned to read and write.

Market Elementary was buzzing with excitement. Teachers had been busy planning Justice Page's visit for weeks. "What an honor to have a visit from his Honor," they gushed. "How special," they fawned as they tidied up their rooms. "Make sure you mind your manners" and "No interrupting" they reminded the students.

MARKET ELEMENTARY
Welcome Justice Page!
Welcome Justice Page
Thanks for coming
Justice

Parents were invited, and they were just as excited as the students and teachers. "I grew up watching him on TV," they told their children as they showed them old football cards and jerseys. "He's in the Hall of Fame!" they beamed. "Be polite" and "Make sure you raise your hand" they reminded their children one last time.

When Alan arrived, he was whisked into the classroom. The students quietly giggled as they watched him lower his towering body onto one of their teeny-tiny chairs.

The gentle bass of Alan's voice carried through the classroom as he began to read. The students leaned forward as they listened to this big man on the tiny chair. All eyes in the classroom were on Alan. All, that is, except for one pair of little boy eyes.

Booker spotted the **perfectly pointy impossibly perpendicular pinky** the moment Alan walked into the classroom and waved. The teachers, parents, and other students also noticed and were curious, but Booker was transfixed.

He knew it would be impolite to ask about it. He knew it was impolite to stare. He knew that he was supposed to sit quietly and listen to Justice Page read. He knew he should just ignore that **perfectly pointy impossibly perpendicular pinky,** but his eyes followed the pinky as though it were a magic wand coming out of the side of the book.

Booker shifted. His knees bounced up and down. He sat up straight. He squirmed. He tried to raise his hand, but he just couldn't hold onto his question any longer.

Booker erupted.

"What happened to your pinky?"

All eyes turned.

Booker, of course.

Booker had a knack for asking inappropriate questions at inappropriate times.

The teachers' eyes narrowed. "Booker!"

The parents' eyes rolled. "Booker!"

The students' eyes widened. "Booker!"

Alan's eyes softened. "Good question, Booker."

Holding up his left hand, Alan asked, "You mean my **perfectly pointy impossibly perpendicular pinky?"**

Alan patiently explained how after years of dislocating his pinky, it eventually stopped working. In the same way that Booker couldn't hold onto his question, the pinky couldn't hold itself straight anymore.

"Does it hurt?" Hazel asked.

"No," Alan replied.

"Aren't you mad?" Felix asked.

"No," Alan said.

"Why don't you fix it?" Ivy asked.

Alan thought about Ivy's question. "It does get in the way," he explained. "It snags on my shirt sleeve when I'm getting dressed. It doesn't cooperate when I put on a glove. And typing on a keyboard can be tricky. But there is one benefit to having a **perfectly pointy impossibly perpendicular pinky,"** he hinted.

Minds raced as everyone tried to figure out what good could come from having a **perfectly pointy impossibly perpendicular pinky.** No one could think of anything. No one, that is, except for Booker.

"I know!" Booker shouted.

All eyes turned toward Booker again.

The teachers' eyes narrowed.

The parents' eyes rolled.

The students' eyes widened.

Everyone held their breath, waiting for Booker to speak.

But Booker didn't speak. He simply grabbed the handlebars of an imaginary bicycle and stuck out his little pinky as far left as he could. Alan smiled. "Booker's got it! You all know about bike safety, right?" Grabbing his own imaginary handlebars and popping out his **perfectly pointy impossibly perpendicular pinky,** he continued. "It makes a really good left-turn signal!"

When his visit was over, Alan waved goodbye. Booker was right up front giving his own special wave back. Remembering himself as a student, Alan gave one last little wave with his **perfectly pointy impossibly perpendicular pinky.**

Booker smiled.

PAGE EDUCATION FOUNDATION

Creating Heroes Through Education & Service

The Page Education Foundation, started by Alan and Diane Page in 1988, assists Minnesota students of color in two ways: Page Scholars get financial help for their post-secondary education, and in turn they spend at least fifty hours each year working with schoolchildren as real-life role models for success. Students at all levels of academic achievement can qualify for a Page Grant, which is awarded based on an applicant's educational goals, willingness to work with children, and financial need. Every student has potential, but many need support to realize their dreams.

Proceeds from the sale of this book help support the Page Education Foundation. To learn more about the Foundation and to order copies of the book, visit www.page-ed.org.

ALAN PAGE is an Associate Justice on the Minnesota State Supreme Court. He was elected to the Court in 1992 and reelected in 1998, 2004, and 2010. He is currently the Court's senior justice.

Alan was a defensive tackle with the Minnesota Vikings and the Chicago Bears from 1967 through 1981. He was selected as the NFL's Most Valuable Player in 1971 and elected to the Pro Football Hall of Fame in 1988.

Alan is an ardent defender of equal education for all children. He is the founder of the Page Education Foundation, founded in 1988, which has awarded more than 8 million dollars in scholarship grants. In 1981 Alan was named one of America's Ten Outstanding Young Men by the United States Jaycees, and in 1991 he received the National Education Association's Friend of Education award.

KAMIE PAGE, Alan's daughter, is a second grade teacher who lives in Minneapolis, Minnesota. She has a Bachelor of Science in Communication from Northwestern University and a Master of Arts in Childhood Education from New York University. Outside of the classroom, she spends most of her time with her husband Ben and their two bright and spunky children, Otis and Esther.

Kamie and Alan share a passion for children's literacy. Kamie's years in the classroom teaching children to read and Alan's years reading books to schoolchildren were the inspirations for this story. This is their first children's book.

Minneapolis artist DAVID GEISTER has shared his passion for art and history with fellow enthusiasts, both young and old, in his paintings for various collectors, historical sites and museums, *The History Channel Magazine*, and several picture books, including *T is for Twin Cities: A Minneapolis/St. Paul Alphabet*, *The Legend of Minnesota*, *Riding to Washington*, and *B is for Battle Cry: A Civil War Alphabet*, which was written by his dear wife, author and teacher Patricia Bauer.

To Otis, Theo, Esther, and Amelia, who are our hope for the future,
and whose days always begin with a book.

And to the more than 5,000 Page Scholars who give meaning to the Page
Education Foundation's motto "Creating Heroes Through Education and Service."
They are our heroes and, through their actions, are making the future better
and brighter.

—A. P. and K. P.

To my dear wife and best friend, Pat. Your passion for teaching,
sharing, and living life to its fullest is my inspiration.

Thank you to Andrew, Ben, Dominic, Grayson, Hanna, Joaquin, and Spencer for
posing as the students in my paintings. I could not have done this without you!

—D. G.

The paintings were rendered in oil paint on gessoed masonite panels.

Text copyright © 2013 Alan Page and Kamie Page
Illustrations copyright © 2013 Book Bridge Press
Illustrations by David Geister
Design by Joe Fahey

NFL-related team names, logos, symbols, uniform designs, or other identifying marks are trademarks of the
National Football League and/or its Member Clubs.

Page Education Foundation
P.O. Box 581254
Minneapolis, MN 55458
www.page-ed.org
info@page-ed.org

Printed and bound in the United States of America

First Edition
Third Printing, 2018

LCCN 2013931662

ISBN 978-0-615-76028-5

This book was expertly produced by Book Bridge Press.
www.bookbridgepress.com